YEEB OF YOR

For Dr. Brandon Mack,

A dear friend and dedicated physician who I know will always be in quest for knowledge in order to help others. May you too also reach for the stars and be greet with happiness.

Susie Cook

7-27-18

Book 3 of the first 10.

PAGE PUBLISHING, INC.
New York, NY

First originally published by Page Publishing, Inc. 2018

ISBN 978-1-64214-106-1 (Paperback)
ISBN 978-1-64214-107-8 (Digital)

Printed in the United States of America

YEEB OF YOR

Susie Cook

1. NORMAL

2 HAPPY

3 UNHAPPY

4 ANGRY

5 SURPRISED
OR
FLUSTERED

6 EMBARRASSED
OR
SHY

FAR BEYOND THE PLANET EARTH
THERE DWELLS THE PLANET YOR.
I guarantee that such a place
You've never seen before.
The Yorians who live there
May look to you quite strange,
Depending on the mood they're in,
Their colors somehow change.

THE CHILDREN ARE CALLED PODREN,
For short they call them pods,
Their parents are called podders,
They call them mums and dodds.

The podren all must go to school,
For this is where they feed.
They must eat all their lessons,
This is how they read.

In a town called Yonder,
There grew a bright young pod,
A constant source of pride he was,
To his mum and dodd,

To him they gave the surname Yeeb,
In Yorish, that meant "learn."
But as you will see, one lesson
Took a twisted turn.

His appetite was endless,
For the knowledge he consumed,
You see he had prepared himself,
For the day he was full bloomed.

ABOARD A FLASHING CRUISER CRAFT

Yeeb departed Planet Yor.
Ever since he was a little pod,
He had wanted to explore.

Yeeb was so excited
He turned an aqua green.
Such wonders he had never ate,
Nor had he ever seen

Traveling the speed of light,
He took time out for a snack.
He was far away from Yor now,
He knew he should head back.

Up ahead he saw a swirl
Of many beams of light.
He knew he had to learn of it,
Or he never would feel right.

But suddenly he felt a force
That changed his shade to red.
This lesson that he hungered for
Was consuming him instead.

HE COULD NOT ESCAPE THE LIGHT BEAMS

That held him in their force.
They were pulling him away from Yor
And from his well-planned course.

After what seemed like forever,
Yeeb landed with a thump.
He was turning a deep purple now,
And feeling like a grump.

At this time, he didn't know.
What might lie in store.
He was quite sure of one thing,
This planet wasn't Yor.

Even though he was full bloomed,
He felt like a little pod.
He reddened once again in fear.
He missed his mum and dodd.

His pointed toes were killing him
And he felt a hunger pain.
Suppose there was no knowledge here,
How on Yor could he maintain?

JUST AS HE WAS LOOSING HOPE,
He heard a greenish noise.
And any pod with any sense
Knew that meant extreme joys.

Picking up his pace again,
He turned a hopeful brown,
What he thought that he was nearing
Was a podrege learning ground.

Unless you've ever been to Yor,
You couldn't even dream
How horrible the noise is
If a Yorian should scream.

What it was that frightened Yeeb
Was how these things appeared,
The strangeness of these creatures
Was surely to be feared.

Just as Yeeb planned to run,
A voice behind him said,
"Hey, Mickey, it's a Martian,
Check out his pointed head!"

11

DESPITE THE REDNESS OF HIS FEAR,
Yeeb took a second look.
To his greenish sheer delight,
One strange pod held a book.

All of Yeeb's hard-eaten knowledge
Can't explain what happened next.
He forgot his fear and gobbled down
The small pod's English text.

Quickly, Yeeb digested
The knowledge he had found.
The podren squealed green noise again
As a hopeful Yeeb turned brown.

Within what seemed the speed of light,
Something strange again occurred.
Before the podren made no sense,
Now he understood each word.

"It must have been that knowledge,"
Yeeb squeaked out high, but clear.
"What kind of podren are you?"
Yeeb asked without a fear.

THEIR FACES' COLOR HADN'T CHANGED

And Yeeb now realized
That these must not be podren,
Regardless of their size.

"Have you any other knowledge,
Perhaps I could consume?
It is knowledge that sustains me.
Without it I face doom."

"There's all the knowledge you can eat,
Right there in that school,"
Mickey kind of smiled and said,
"Please eat until you're full!"

"Don't let the teacher see you.
She'll really lay an egg!
She'll chew you up and spit you out,
And I'm not pulling your leg."

Yeeb turned so red he thought that he
Might fade right then and there.
These "beings" could be violent,
He would have to be aware.

DESPITE HIS FEAR OF BEING CHEWED,
Yeeb knew he had to try,
If he could just eat the right knowledge,
He could make his cruiser fly.

When the podren-looking beings
Said they would assist,
He knew it was an offer
That he could not resist.

"Let's just wait until the bell,
Then we'll be set to go.
If we wait until everyone else has left,
No one will ever know."

A sound rang out that sounded like
A podrege dinner bell.
A brown-and-tannish Yeeb then smiled.
Now things were going well.

Once the school was empty,
They simply slipped inside.
"We'll show you where the books are kept,
Then we'll go out and hide."

YEEB LOOKED AROUND AT ALL THE BOOKS.
There were hundreds here at least.
He turned a bright and grateful green
And then began his feast.

Yeeb ate and snacked for hours,
Until his head was full.
There was sure a lot of knowledge
Stored inside this school!

He understood this planet,
Must be the planet Earth.
At least he knew right where he was,
Whatever that was worth.

He now knew about these beings,
They were called the human race.
There were good ones and some bad ones
That was true of any place.

On Yor there were "unlearners"—
They only ate bad news.
They were cast away and never knew
The joy of aqua blues.

THEIR COLORS NEVER CHANGED AT ALL,
Reddish purple were their moods.
So limited on Yor they were.
They ignored the knowledge foods.

But here and now was where Yeeb was,
And he had to find his path,
Using geography with science,
He could apply his math.

Yeeb had learned his newfound friends
On Earth were called young boys.
He knew that they were nearing
For he heard a greenish noise.

The young boys bounded in the room
To see how Yeeb had done.
They were really overjoyed to see,
He ate every book but one.

Then Mickey said, "Hey, Mortie,
We're really off the hook.
They can't make us do our lessons
If we don't have any books!"

THEN YEEB TURNED REALLY YELLOW,
His shade for being sad.
"I didn't know this knowledge
Was all you young boys had."

"Don't worry, Yeeb, this isn't stuff
We'll ever have to know."
We have all the knowledge we might need,
For where we have to go.

A greener Yeeb said, "Well okay,
Now I guess I must prepare.
Thanks to all your knowledge.
I can begin my craft's repair."

"You must be kidding, surely, Yeeb.
You couldn't know much more
About fixing up your cruiser craft,
Than you did before."

"No, Mickey," Yeeb quite greenly said.
"I have an understanding
Of what it was that brought me here
And caused my sudden landing."

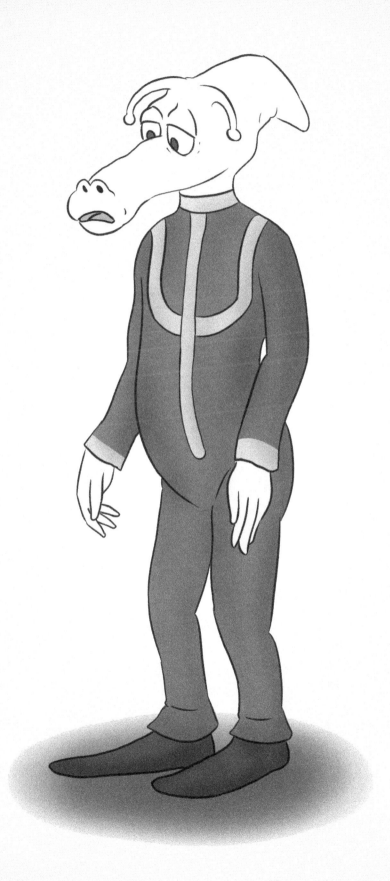

"TRAPPED WITHIN THE SPEED OF LIGHT,
I crossed the speed of sound,
My time meter was thrown astray
And gravity brought me down.

"Once I reset all my gauges,
And knock out just one dent,
By tomorrow you'll be saying,
'It was off to Yor, Yeeb went.'"

"Can we go with you to your craft?
We'll do everything we can!"
"Of course," a grateful green Yeeb said.
"You can help me with my plan."

The boys were really quite impressed
With Yeeb's crashed up cruiser.
"Boy, Yeeb, you're lucky you weren't hurt.
This could have been a bruiser!"

Despite the boy's confusing words,
Yeeb kind of understood.
Even though he'd crashed the cruiser,
His landing had been good.

THE BOYS SAID THEY COULD FIX THE DENT.
They were really good with tools.
With a hammer and a bender
And a few good push and pulls.

Yeeb began with all the gauges.
There must have been fifteen.
He turned every color know to Yor
Until alas he did turn green.

Within a few short hours,
The cruiser was like new.
Yeeb then turned a hopeful brown
But the boys said they felt blue.

Yeeb said, "Gee, that's funny.
You look the same shade to me."
The boys said when they saddened
It wasn't plain to see.

"I'm sorry, boys, I have to fly.
It also turns me blue.
My podders must be worried,
And it's what I have to do."

"OUR PARENTS TOO WILL WONDER,
Where on Earth we're at.
We're usually home by four o'clock
And it's way after that."

Yeeb jumped in behind the wheel,
And smiled a green-blue smile.
Earth's knowledge has been scary
But all-in-all worthwhile.

The boys then shouted loud to Yeeb,
"From now on, we will learn.
We'll find you someday out there, Yeeb,
We've got no time to burn."

Yeeb understood each single word
And smiled a hopeful brown.
Such wonders he'd never eaten,
Nor had he ever found.

With a loud sudden blast,
Yeeb departed Planet Earth.
He's gained a lot of knowledge here,
And he knew what that was worth!

HE WOULD TAKE THIS KNOWLEDGE BACK TO YOR

And write it in a book,
All of Yor would then consume,
Perhaps his mum would cook.

The young boys stared into the sky
Until Yeeb disappeared.
They laughed at how they now loved books
That once they might have feared.

Someday they'd travel far to Yor.
Yeeb would turn so green.
Such wonders they had never read,
Nor had they ever seen.

THE END

About the Author

Newly-published Susie Cook is a lifelong writer who attributes her gift of writing as a gift from God. From the time she learned to write, she has entertained friends and family with her stories and poetry almost entirely in rhyme. As a young fan of Dr. Seuss, Susie found words that rhyme stay with a person. Susie's writing ranges from short stories to personalized greeting cards, and she is always looking for a positive and humorous spin to mesmerize and thrill her readers. Susie finds writing to be her way of traveling to places she can only dream of. Travel with her to Yor and back again. If you enjoy your travels, watch for more from Susie Cook. Susie would love to mesmerize and thrill you with her gift from God to you in the future.

CPSIA information can be obtained
at www.ICGtesting.com
Printed in the USA
BVHW02s0600190718
522011BV00007B/21/P

9 781642 141061